Contents

D0956587

Chapter 1

Rosie Lockett was rocket crazy. She had rockets on her dresses, rockets on her jeans, rockets on her socks.

She read about rockets, she wrote about rockets, she talked about nothing else but rockets.

Then, one day, her parents cried out, "Rosie Lockett, that's enough about rockets!"

Rosie was silent – for about a second. Then, as quick as a rocket, she said, "Well, what else can I talk about?"

"Anything but rockets!" they said.

So Rosie entered contests,
every kind of contest, but, sadly,
Rosie never, ever won any of them.
She didn't mind at all though.
She just loved giving them a try.

Then, one morning, she found out about yet another contest.

"Hello, Rosie," said the mail carrier. "Won any contests yet?"

"Not yet," she replied.

"Well, why don't you enter the annual post office contest?" he said. "It looks for the wackiest mailbox in town."

Rosie stared at her mailbox.
It was a plain box on a plain pole.

"Not wacky, is it?" she said.

"No," laughed the mail carrier,
as he rested by Rosie's mailbox.

"Oh, I nearly forgot," he said.
"This year, the street with the
greatest number of wacky mailboxes
wins a prize, too."

A little while later, Rosie's neighbor, Mr. Slater, came over to see what all the clanging and banging was about.

"What's up?" he asked.

"I'm going to build a mailbox," replied Rosie.

"What's wrong with the one you have?"

"Nothing, it's just not very wacky," she said.

Then she started telling him about the contest. Soon everyone on her street, Peach Parade, had heard about it, too. They were all as excited as Rosie to build wacky mailboxes.

In no time at all, there was clanging and banging coming from every yard on the street.

Several hours later, Mr. Slater came over to Rosie's yard again. He saw Rosie standing outside a tent.

"Going camping?" he asked.

"No, I'm going to build my mailbox inside my tent," she said. "I don't want anyone to see what mine is going to look like. It's going to be a secret."

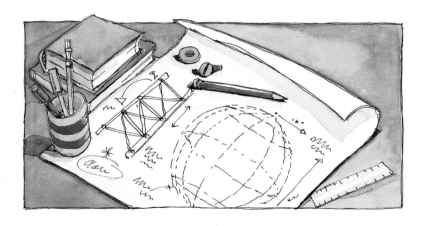

"Great, I love surprises!" said Mr. Slater, and he went back to building his lighthouse mailbox.

Chapter 2

Peach Parade had always been
a quiet street, but not anymore.
Everyone was rushing around
with boxes of nails and screws,
planks of wood, and cans of paint.

The mail carrier had always
put letters into mailboxes, but not
anymore. Every mailbox on Peach
Parade was now just a cardboard
box with a cutout hole and
a handwritten number.

"Don't worry," Rosie told the mail
carrier. "Soon you'll put our letters
in the wackiest mailboxes in town."

On the morning of the contest, Peach Parade was closed to the public so that no one could see the mailboxes.

To make it more fun, everyone on Peach Parade dressed up to match the theme of their mailbox.

At Number 1, Mr. Green stood
by his submarine mailbox dressed
in a blue sailor suit.

Across the street, Mrs. Tripp wore
pirate clothes. Her pirate ship mailbox
had a number two stitched on a sail.

The mailbox at Number 3
was a castle with turrets and
a paddling-pool moat. Mr. Beckett
stood by his mailbox in a knight's
costume of shining armor.

"The mail goes in here,"
he explained, as he opened
the drawbridge and put in a letter.

At Number 4, Mrs. Weatherspoon was dressed as a Japanese doll. Her mailbox was a dollhouse.

At Number 5, five candles sat on top of the five-layer fudge cake mailbox. Mrs. Lopez's mailbox and lollipop chef's hat looked good enough to eat.

Mr. Slater's lighthouse mailbox
at Number 6 looked great, and so
did Mr. Slater in his yellow raincoat
and hat. However, it was Rosie's tent
that everyone stopped to stare at.

"Sorry, it's still a surprise," she said.

"Excuse me, folks," cried
Mr. Beckett, "the judges aren't
here yet, but they soon will be.
Back to your houses, please."

So everyone dashed off to stand
by their mailboxes.

Chapter 3

For the people of Peach Parade,
the wait was nearly over. The two
judges were only one street away.
This was Rosie's signal to start
getting ready. She went inside
the tent, changed into her costume,
and put the finishing touches
to her mailbox.

Everyone on Peach Parade gathered
around to watch as Rosie took
down her tent, revealing her mailbox.
When people saw what she had
made, they just stood and stared.
It was truly out of this world!

Moments later, the judges marched onto Peach Parade, went up to Mr. Green's submarine mailbox, and started making notes. Their faces didn't give anything away as they rated everyone's mailbox.

Finally, they walked over to Rosie's mailbox, the last to be judged in the contest. At her front walk, they just stopped and gaped for several minutes. Then they started whispering wildly to each other.

Chapter 4

Not long after that, the judges walked over to the microphone.

"We'd like to say how much we loved all the mailboxes," said the first judge. "But every contest must have a winner. So the special prize for the street with the greatest number of wacky mailboxes goes to..."

The second judge leaned toward the microphone.

"Peach Parade!"

The crowd cheered and clapped.

Then the first judge continued,
"The post office has decided to print
a stamp series of wacky mailboxes.
Pictures of the Peach Parade
mailboxes will appear on every
letter and parcel in the country."
The crowd cheered and clapped.

"And now the part you've all been waiting for," said the first judge. "May I say that we've found it hard to choose the most wacky mailbox. But, after a lot of thought, we've made our choice."

The crowd was so quiet you could have heard a letter drop.

The second judge leaned toward the microphone once again.

"First prize, for the overall winner of the post office's sixth annual mailbox contest, goes to..."
He paused. "Rosie Lockett of Number 7 Peach Parade for her out-of-this-world rocket mailbox!"

The crowd cheered and clapped.

While Rosie was making her way over to the judges, Mrs. Lopez rushed past, carrying a huge cake for the street party afterward.

However, as she passed Rosie's mailbox, a gust of wind blew a spark from one of the candles and lit the rocket fireworks on Rosie's mailbox. The next thing everyone knew, Rosie was counting down into the microphone, "3, 2, 1... Liftoff!"

As people ran and dived for cover, Rosie made a short speech.

"I've never been first in my life," said Rosie. "But now I've been first twice in one day. First in the contest, and maybe my mailbox will be the first mailbox to land on the moon!"

Everyone laughed and laughed.

Chapter 5

Soon, everything was back to normal on Peach Parade. Well... almost. Rosie had put her rocket mailbox back together, but the mail carrier was never on time again. He couldn't help playing with the mailboxes, even on the days when the people didn't get any mail.

A month after the contest, the mail carrier knocked on Rosie's door.

"Special delivery for Rosie Lockett!" he announced.

Rosie took a letter out of his hand. There, in all its glory, was Rosie's rocket stamp.

After that, it didn't take Rosie long to find something else to do with her spare time. She's now crazy about stamps. She just loves the ones of the Peach Parade wacky mailboxes. But her favorite stamps are, of course, the ones of *rockets!*

From the Author

I'd love to be Peach Parade's mail carrier. Imagine giving a phone bill to a pirate who could pay with gold doubloons! As a child, I, too, used to tackle tasks with the force of a rocket. My mother would have to do a countdown and wait for me to make a touchdown on Earth!

Janine Scott

From the Illustrator

I hope you enjoy Rosie's adventures on Peach Parade. She's very passionate about things that interest her, and I love the way her enthusiasm inspires everyone on the street to do the best job they can. Rosie is a motivator. They are my favorite kind of people.

John Bennett

If you have enjoyed reading
3, 2, 1, *Liftoff!*
read these other Storyteller Chapter Books.

Crazy Miss Maisey's Alphabet Pets
The Flutey Family Fruitcake
Rupert Goes to School
Feathers
Coyote, Fox, and Wolf Tales
Happily Ever After!
No Space to Waste
Those Birds!
Pandora's Box
Sam's Dad
Birds of Prey
Bird Watchers
Zoom In!
Clever Coyote and Other Wild Dogs
Trees, Please!
Solve This!